The CHRISTMAS TREE that Ate My Mother

The Christmas Tree that Ate My Mother

Dean Marney

AN
APPLE
PAPERBACK

SCHOLASTIC INC.
New York Toronto London Auckland Sydney

ISBN 0-590-44881-1

12 11 10 9 8 7 6 5 4 3   2 3 4 5 6 7/9

Printed in the U.S.A.   28

First Scholastic printing, October 1992

For Blythe

✳ 1 ✳

My little brother has a rubber-cement booger collection. He keeps it under his bed in a tennis-shoe box. He has one of every size. He says he loves rubber-cement boogers, and just between you and me, whether he admits it or not, he likes the real ones, too.

It is what I gave him for Christmas, rubber cement, not boogers. I'm telling the truth. It is what I give him every year. It's always his favorite present.

My name is Elizabeth but everyone calls me Lizzie, and my brother's name is Booger when my parents can't hear you and Booker when they can. He's in third grade and he's weird.

I'm in the fifth grade, and right now I'm wearing my favorite pair of jeans and my new T-shirt that says WILD WOMEN DON'T GET THE BLUES on it. The shirt was a gift from my cousin and the words are true, sort of. I get in trouble a lot. Right this minute I also smell wild. I'm wearing this perfume my mom doesn't want anymore, and it's really gross, but I kind of like it.

I actually never really knew what wild was until this last Christmas. You want wild? See how you like this for a Christmas.

Here is how it started. Christmas was only a couple of days away. I was starting to get what my dad calls the Christmas crazies. It's like you get real hyper and excited about Christmas, but you also get mad and cranky a lot and get in trouble. I was in trouble at the moment for not having my hair washed. I didn't think it looked so bad.

I think washing your hair is about the most boring thing you can do. It takes forever and I can never get the soap out.

My mother keeps saying, "Cut it short and it will be much easier to take care of."

I always reply, "Over my dead body."

We were about to leave to go get our Christmas tree. Every year we are the absolute last people in the world to get one.

I told Dad, "As usual the only ones left will be totally dry, short, and extremely ugly."

He said, "The only ones left will be magic." He opened his eyes real wide. My dad is sort of weird anyway, but Christmas makes him even weirder.

"What do you mean?" I asked. "Where are you taking us?"

"I don't mean anything," he said.

He knew I didn't believe him. I squinted my

eyes at him like I was trying to see into his brain.

"Okay," he said. "I heard there is a new lot in town, and maybe we'll go check it out."

"Great," I said. "It's going to be another terrific year of Christmas tree hunting for Lizzie."

My dad insists on looking at every lot, in and out of town, till you just want to puke, literally.

"I bet this new lot is three trillion miles away."

"Be positive," said my dad. He was whistling "Joy to the World."

"Why can't we just go to the mall and buy the first tree we see? All the good ones are taken anyway."

He didn't answer me.

The reason we are the last ones to go get our Christmas tree is because my mother is a fanatic about not rushing the season.

"How can you rush it," I said, "when it is practically over before we start?"

"When you're grown-up and have a place of your own," said my mother, "you can put your tree up during Halloween if you'd like."

"I will," I said. "I may put it up and leave it up year round."

"That's nice, dear," she said.

The only decorations we have up are an Advent calendar and an Advent wreath. We have them only because my mother says the season is really Advent until Christmas Eve, so Advent things are okay.

3

I told her, "Advent calendars are not decorations. They are baby stuff and boring, especially when you have to take turns opening the doors with your brother."

She said, "It seems to me that sharing has something to do with the Advent season."

"Boring," I said.

4

❄ **2** ❄

We drove to a Christmas tree lot my mom said she liked, close to our house. Well, it was only three miles away. Every tree was short and ugly. I sang, "I told you so," to the tune of "Jingle Bells" in the backseat.

"Lizzie, you're making this *not* fun," my mom said.

I'm the one in the family that makes things *not* fun, always. I can't help myself. My mom says, "You're going down the wrong road, Elizabeth. Choose the good road not the bad, please."

The problem is that a part of me just loves to go down the bad road. Everyone knows I'm stubborn, and they always say I don't know when to quit.

"I'm just singing," I said. "Can't I even sing?"

"No," my mother said.

"Great," I said, "I'll never sing again." I started humming.

We tried two other lots with no luck. The trees

were taller but drier than the desert. My mom kept saying, "Fire hazard," at each one we looked at. If she said it one more time I was going to scream.

I said to my mother, "We have a smoke alarm and we could buy a fire extinguisher."

At the next lot my parents thought the trees didn't have enough branches.

I said, "I don't know about you, but I'm beginning to hate Christmas. How many branches do you need?"

My mother threatened to leave me there. I thought about it seriously for a couple of minutes, but decided against it. Then Booger managed to get himself lost. He is so stupid. I was mad at my parents because we had a chance to leave *him* there, and they weren't taking it.

I very politely asked, "Why don't we just leave him here?"

My mom told me I'd better wait in the car.

I waited in the car forever. They couldn't find him. I knew the little creep was hiding.

I finally rolled down the car window and yelled, "Booker, they gave us free candy."

It was a complete lie but he bought it. He came running to the car. Get this though, I got in trouble for lying. He didn't get in trouble at all. My parents are insane.

Then my dad said he knew the perfect place to

get the perfect tree, and winked at me. We were going to his new place.

"If we had to go there anyway, why didn't we go there first and get it over with?" I asked.

"Liz," said my dad, "try to have fun."

How could I have fun? It had been freezing cold when we left the house, so I had put on practically every piece of clothing I owned. Since then, the sun had come out, and we had gotten in and out of the hot car six million times looking at fire hazards and trees with no limbs. We also got to look for Booger and, with my typical luck, we found him.

I was itchy, hot, cranky and if I had to go to one more lot I was going to puke, literally. I saw a bunch of artificial trees standing in the corner of the lot under a blue-and-white canopy.

"Since we wait so long every year, why don't we just buy an artificial tree?" I asked.

"We could," said my dad, "it just . . ."

"Wouldn't be the same," finished my mom.

"I'm going to die," I said.

"Elizabeth," said my mother, "what road are you going down?"

"A very long one."

We drove some more. I got into a fight with Booger because he was saying *beep* all the time.

I'd say, "Quit it, please. You're driving me crazy," and all he'd say was *beep* or *beep beep*.

I complained to my dad but he said *beep*, too.

"Great," I said, but I didn't mean it.

Then my dad pulled into a lot with this sign over the entrance: RALPH'S MAGIC CHRISTMAS TREES.

"Now we're talking," said my dad.

My mom said, "Look at all these trees. They are so thick, you could get lost in them."

I had a funny feeling when we drove into the lot, and it wasn't carsickness.

❄ 3 ❄

R alph was weirder than my dad, and his trees didn't look all that magic to me. You could say one thing for them though, they weren't short and they weren't dry. Ralph acted like he knew us. I thought it was real irritating. He acted as if he were expecting us.

I detest it when people pretend like they've known you their whole life and act like you're their best friend just to get something from you. There's this guy at school. He's cute but he's only nice to me — he only acts like he knows me — when he wants to borrow money for the candy machine.

I just didn't trust Ralph. He was being all nicey-nice to my parents though, and they were eating it up. Parents are suckers for niceness.

Ralph, with a smooth-as-cream voice, said, "Your tree is waiting for you right over here."

You should have seen my mother just hustle

right over there, like it was the major sale of the year. It was disgusting.

Booger said, "Really, a tree has been waiting for us? Is it magic?" He totally believed Ralph.

I couldn't believe that he was that dumb. I was totally embarrassed. However, what did I expect? I once sold him rocks and told him if he sucked on them they'd turn into candy. He sucked on them forever. Every time he'd start to give up I'd tell him to just keep working on them and they'd turn to candy. He believed me for a whole day. I think my mom finally had to make him stop, and, of course, I got in trouble because he was so stupid.

"You know," said Ralph. "You buy this tree at your own risk."

My mom and dad laughed.

Real funny, I thought.

Ralph acted weird, but there was something else strange about him that I couldn't put my finger on. His clothes were ridiculous. They were normal clothes. He had on khaki pants, a blue sweater, and one of those Santa hats. They just didn't look normal on *him*.

He looked like he'd borrowed them from someone. They just didn't fit who he looked like. He looked as if he were wearing a costume.

The thought came into my head that he was probably an alien who'd stolen the clothes. He was a big guy. He wasn't fat. He was tall and muscular. He was older than my dad. I couldn't tell how old. He did have a beard, though, and it was partially gray.

He showed us the tree. It was about eight feet tall, my dad told us, and Ralph said he was right. It was super thick and very green, not a brown needle on it. It looked really good.

"It's so fresh and green," said Ralph, "you could leave it up year round." He winked at me.

"Can we go somewhere else?" I whispered to my dad.

I didn't think Ralph had heard me. I didn't think my dad had even heard me.

Ralph said, "Lizzie is strong and knows what to do."

He knew my name and no one had told him. I was ticked. I started to ask him how he knew so dang much when I'd never met him before in my life, but my dad was too busy asking him how much the tree cost.

Ralph said, "Let me see how much this one is." He started moving branches looking for a tag. As he did that I thought I saw something.

It was very quick, but I thought I saw something bright-white move between the branches. It was like someone had opened a small window and thrown a bolt of lightning out of it.

"What was that?" I asked.

"Did you see something?" said Ralph.

"I don't know," I said.

11

"What are you talking about?" asked Booger.

"I just thought I saw something in the tree," I said.

"Probably a bird," my dad said.

"No," I said, "it wasn't a bird."

"It's a magic tree just for you," said Ralph. "Take it home and it will show you lots of things." He looked straight at me and laughed.

Booger poked me and whispered, "Why did he say that to you?"

"Don't ask me," I said.

Ralph told my dad how much the tree was, and we couldn't believe it. It was discounted or something.

"Dad, there's something wrong with it. No tree is that cheap."

In typical fashion he didn't listen to me. No one ever listens to me. I don't count.

My dad paid for the tree, and we tied it to the top of our car. As we were just pulling out, Ralph came running over and tapped on my window.

I rolled it down and he said to all of us, "Have a Merry Christmas," and then just to me he said, "Lizzie, don't be afraid of the dark."

My dad turned out of the lot and we started home.

"Strange guy," said my dad, "but I knew it was going to be a great lot."

"He kind of gives me the creeps," I said. "I think he's an ax-killer."

"Really, Lizzie, try to be a little trusting," said my mom.

My dad said, "You're watching too much TV, Liz. Way too much."

"He seemed nice enough," said my mom, "but there was something a little odd about him. It really seemed like he was expecting us."

"Oh, well," said my dad, "lots of people are strange."

"Especially at Christmas," said my mom.

"No kidding," I said, looking right at Booger.

"And," said my dad, "we now have a beautiful tree."

My mom said, "We'll be home in time for us to have lunch. Then the kids and I can go to pageant practice, and you can get the tree ready to decorate."

"Sounds fair," said my dad.

"Can't I stay with Dad?" I asked.

"You have to go to pageant practice," my mom replied.

"Why?" I asked. "I hate pageant practice. It's so stupid. You do the same story every year. The same thing happens. The kids even make the same mistakes every year. Besides, I'm too old to be in the pageant. It's embarrassing."

"I'm sorry," said my mother. "You're my daughter. I'm in charge of the pageant and I need your help. The subject is closed, or would you like to discuss calling off Christmas this year?"

"Great," I said, and I almost meant it.

❋ 4 ❋

Pageant practice was embarrassing. I felt just too old for pageants. I was right about it being the same script, too. Everything was the same. It was the same church, the same kids, except maybe one or two new ones. We just got different parts from last year.

The characters would have been the same, too, except my mother had to add a character at the last minute. She had to add someone to walk around with the Blessed Virgin Mary and help her with her lines because they asked the dumbest girl in the world to play Mary.

Guess who got to be the new character? You guessed it. Me. That's what you get when your mother is in charge.

I wanted to be the Angel of the Lord. I played it last year and was terrific. You have to hide up by the altar, and then jump up on a stool and scare the shepherds, and then tell them, "Don't be afraid." Father Tlucek told my mother I was the scariest Angel of the Lord he'd ever seen.

My mother told me, "Not this year. Mary needs your help."

"Mary needs to learn to read," I said.

"I'm counting on you," my mother said.

"Mother," I said, "there is no real part for someone to follow Mary around, except maybe a donkey, and I'm not going to be a donkey."

"Fine," said my mother, "you can be Mary's friend. You're her helper. Mary certainly had friends."

"How do you know?" I asked.

"Women have friends," my mother said. "Trust me."

"I don't even have a name," I said. "I suppose my name is Mary's friend."

"I've got it," said my mom. "Who's every girl's best friend?"

"Her dog?" I answered.

"No, you creep," she said. "It's her mother." She then hugged me in front of everyone. "You can be Mary's mother, Saint Anne."

"Did she go to Bethlehem with her?" I asked.

"Well, if she didn't, she wanted to."

I stood there for a minute and thought about it. "Oh, all right." I said it like I didn't really want to do it, but I sort of liked the idea of being a saint. I figured that if I had to follow Mary around I might as well be a saint. It beat being a donkey.

We practiced. Louise was Mary, and I had to

tell her everything to say and do. She didn't know anything. She got to be Mary because everybody is supposed to feel sorry for her because her mother is getting divorced for about the fiftieth time.

She was so stupid. She even had the nerve to ask me why I was following her around. I don't know why I bothered, but I tried to be nice and not say, "Because you're dumb." I told her it was because I was her mother.

She said, "Mary didn't have a mother."

"Everyone's got a mother," I said. "My name is Saint Anne, and if you don't stop getting on my nerves, I'm going to give you the worst bloody nose you've ever had in your life."

She shut up after that.

We went through the whole thing three times until I thought I was going to drop, and then we had to do it once more with music.

Finally my mother said everything looked wonderful and, "Be here early Christmas Eve to get your costumes on." She then offered a sheet with the words to the songs for the people who didn't already know them.

Almost nobody needed them. We've sung the same songs since I can remember, and if you don't know "Silent Night" and "Away in a Manger" by now, something is wrong with you. Well, guess who didn't know them. Louise asked for the words.

❄ 5 ❄

By the time we got home my dad had the tree up. It wasn't in the usual place over by the window, and my dad had rearranged all the living room furniture. I could tell my mother didn't like it.

"Funny thing about this tree," he said.

Mom asked, "Why did you put it over there?" She acted kind of mad.

"I'm telling you," he answered, "it's a weird tree. It just wouldn't go in the regular place."

"Phil, the kids wore me out. What do you mean?"

"I mean," said my dad, "I mean . . . I don't know what I mean. I just tried to put it over there by the window, but every time I did, I ended up over here by the staircase."

"Phil, that's ridiculous. If you want it over by the stairs, just say so. You don't have to make up a story."

My dad looked at both Booger and me and tried

to look serious so we'd believe him, but then he started laughing.

"I swear," he said, "I am not lying. The tree will not go over by the window."

"Then why are you laughing?" asked Booger.

"Excellent example for the children, Phil," said my mother.

"Fine," said my dad, and he wasn't laughing now. "You try it. You'll see."

"All right, I will," said my mother.

"You won't be able to lift it," I said.

She turned to me, snapping my head off, and said, "Thanks for the vote of confidence, Lizzie."

My mom looked up to the top of the tree and then tried to peek around it.

"It looks so much bigger in the house than it did on the lot," she said. "How did you ever get it in the door?"

"It wanted to come into the house," said my dad.

My mom glared at him.

"I'll help you, Mom," said Booger.

She looked at me.

"Don't look at me," I said. "I like it right where it is."

"Some friend you are," she said.

I thought for a minute, and then I figured it was too close to Christmas not to do your mother a favor.

"Okay, fine," I said, "I'll help. Otherwise I'll be in trouble for the rest of my life."

"If Lizzie is going to help then I'll help, too," said my dad.

"No funny stuff," said my mom to my dad.

"No funny stuff," Booger said to me.

"You make me sick," I whispered to him.

We each found a place to grab the trunk of the tree. I couldn't see a thing because I had two branches poking me in the eyes.

"When I say three," said my mom, "we'll carry it toward Dad and put it in front of the window. Okay?"

"Okay," we all said.

"One, two, three," said my mom.

We picked it up and, as we started across the room, it felt like everything was fine.

"Can you see where we are?" asked my mom.

"I'm against the window," said my dad.

"Okay," said my mom, "put it down."

We put it down and stepped back. My mother screamed, not a real scream but a kind of wimp scream. We had put the tree down exactly where we had started from.

She was really mad at my dad.

"Phil," she said, "this isn't funny."

My dad was laughing again. He tried to stop.

"I'm sorry," he said, "I just don't get it. It did the same thing to me."

My mother almost popped her eyes out glaring at my dad.

"Everyone get out of my way," she said. "I'll do it myself."

"I'll help," said Booger.

"Shut up," I said.

"Mom," he said.

"Knock it off you two," she said. "Everyone get out of my way."

We stood back, and my mom took a huge breath and practically dove into the center of the tree. We could barely see her, and she couldn't have been able to see anything.

"Tell me when I'm there," she said.

Then she grunted real loud and sort of lifted but mostly dragged the tree toward the window. She looked like she was dancing and wrestling with the tree at the same time.

"Am I there?" she yelled.

"Almost," I said, "about three more feet. Okay, fine, you're there. Set it down."

But instead of setting it down she picked up the tree and ran all the way back across the room with it and then set it down. She came out from the center of the tree and really screamed this time.

"Phil," she said, "*what* is going on?"

Booger said, "It's magic."

I said, "This is giving me the creeps."

We all stood and looked at the tree.

My mom finally started laughing hysterically. I

thought she'd completely flipped out. I was ready to dial 911 and say there was a crazy woman at our house.

She then went up to my dad and hugged him and said, "Phil, I don't know how you did it, but you're such a practical joker."

Booger started laughing at Dad like he'd done something funny. I didn't get it.

My mom stepped back and looked the tree up and down.

She said, "I like it here. Phil, you're right. It belongs right where it is."

My dad looked like he was in partial shock.

He started to say, "But I didn't . . ."

My mom didn't hear him. She was now in the closet digging out our Christmas ornaments.

"Dad?" I asked. "Did you really move the tree the whole time? If you did, how'd you do it?"

He shrugged his shoulders at me.

"I don't know, Liz, but I must have done it."

He stood thinking for a minute.

"I guess," he said, "I always wanted the tree by the stairs."

❄ 6 ❄

I don't like winter. I'm a summer girl. I hate it getting dark so early in the day and I hate getting up in the morning while it's still dark. I'm not really fond of the dark.

Most people are afraid of the dark. Well, I am, too, sort of. I'll take light any day over dark. I'm in the fifth grade and I sleep with a night-light on, and I don't care who knows it.

What makes me mad is that when you were little and you said you were afraid of the dark, people always asked you why. I didn't know why and I still don't. I was just afraid. I like to be able to see things. I prefer lights.

So, here it is Christmas. The season to drive your family crazy so they can drive you crazy. There's lots to not like about Christmas, but you can't say anything or everyone will jump down your throat.

Adults can complain about Christmas and they

do it all the time. They say, "It's too busy. I don't have enough time. It's so commercial."

However, if a kid complains about Christmas it's like they just murdered Santa Claus. Kids are supposed to love everything about Christmas. They're supposed to love being fed a ton of sugar and yelled at for being hyper. They're supposed to be all excited about getting presents but not be disappointed when they don't get a thing that they wanted.

Don't get me wrong. I like Christmas, most of it. It's just that nothing is perfect.

Sometimes I'd just like to say to adults, "We're not stupid," and have them believe me.

So, I'm being negative. I'm sorry. Put me in jail.

Like I said, even with crazy parents and a dork for a brother, I still like Christmas. I think that's being very positive.

I just don't get all weird about the stuff I do like. I just don't make a big deal out of it. I like that it's a season of lights. Everyone puts up lights outside and inside and we light candles. It isn't just Christmas either. Hanukkah is the celebration of lights. For someone who doesn't particularly like the dark, it's a nice touch.

I lifted the tree lights out of the Christmas decoration box and plugged them in.

"Who-e-e-e," said my dad.

There were about four hundred thousand light

bulbs out. We had to replace them all before we could string them on the tree. Booger kept telling me to hurry up until I just wanted to slap him silly, but my mother was too close to us.

I finally said to him, "Why don't you try screwing them in with your mouth zipped shut, you moron."

"Lizzie," my mom said, "I can't believe the way you talk to him. It embarrasses me."

"Fine," I said, "you're always on his side."

"Liz, don't start in," said my dad.

"Would everyone please get off my back?" I said.

"It just seems," said my mother, not even looking at me, "that every time we're trying to do something together, you refuse to just let things be. You always have to get in a fight, and then you don't know when to quit. Why can't we just all get along? Why can't you be agreeable just once in a while."

I started yelling, "You hate me. You're always telling me I'm wrong."

There was nothing but silence.

"Let's just start over," said my mother.

"Great," said my dad. "Everyone get under control, and let's not say anything *to* or *about* someone unless it's nice."

"Fine with me," I said. I decided I wasn't going to say anything, especially not to Booger or my

24

mother, who I decided probably wasn't my real mother.

Then I looked at the stupid tree. I didn't know if it was because we were fighting, but looking at the tree made me feel funny. It made me feel sad. I also felt a tingling feeling in my legs and arms.

Great, I thought, I'm probably getting sick. I'll be in trouble for that, too.

The string of lights was fully lit now and my dad wound them around the tree. "Higher, Phil," my mother kept saying. "Space them out."

When he finished, Booger and I and Mom started decorating. I got in trouble again. This time it was for moving every decoration Booger put on, but I couldn't help it. He put them in the dumbest places.

My mother said, "Lizzie, if you move another ornament, you don't get to help."

"But he's ruining the tree. He puts everything in the wrong place."

My mother gritted her teeth and said, "Try for once to be agreeable, Elizabeth."

"Fine," I said, "if you want an ugly tree, I don't care."

About ten minutes passed and Booger said, "She's moving them again."

I said, "I swear I'm not."

"Liz, I mean it," my mom said. "You've gone too far. You never know when to quit."

"I swear," I said. "I didn't touch them."

"Then who did?" said Booger.

"I didn't," I said to my dad, trying to get him on my side.

Then I noticed something. The ornament I had just put on the tree was moved.

"Who is moving my ornaments?" I asked.

"She's only trying to act innocent," said Booger.

"I mean it," I said. "Someone else is moving the ornaments."

We all looked at my dad.

"Will you all stop looking at me?" he said. "It isn't me."

❄ 7 ❄

T hat's it," said my dad, "looks finished to me."
"There are no more decorations," said
Booger. He was standing there picking his nose.

"Do you think you're going to find some in
there?" I asked him.

My dad thought I was funny, but he tried not
to laugh.

"Elizabeth," he said, "cut it out."

"He makes me sick," I said.

"Just stop," my dad said. "Quit for once."

For just a second, the lights on the Christmas
tree went out and then they came back on. We
all looked at my mom. Something was wrong with
her. She looked really funny. She was like doing
aerobics with her lips.

I started laughing. I couldn't help it. I mean
she looked really weird. I don't even know how
she could do that with her lips. She finally put her
hands over her mouth.

"What's wrong, honey?" asked my dad.

"I don't know," said my mother.

"Maybe you should sit down," said my dad.

My mom sat down on the couch and she stopped doing her lip thing.

"Are you okay?" said my dad.

"I don't know what happened, Phil," she said. "I was just standing there and my lips started acting weird. I must be completely stressed out. I guess I'm just tired."

"Do you feel sick?" asked my dad.

My mom was sitting there sort of staring into space.

We all stood around her not knowing what to say or do. She looked at Booger and me and made herself laugh.

She said, "I'm going to bed early tonight. That's a promise."

I accidentally bumped into Booger. He acted like he'd just been run over by a garbage truck.

"Knock it off," said Booger.

"It was an accident," I said.

"Knock it off, both of you, now," said my dad. He was cranky but his lips were normal.

We looked at the tree.

My mother said, "It's the most beautiful tree I've ever seen."

She was right but I didn't like it. There was something about that tree.

Booger said, "We forgot the angel. It doesn't have a top."

I found it at the bottom of the decoration box. There she was, wrapped in tissue paper in a plastic bag. I took her out carefully. She smelled sort of like herbal tea.

Booger said, "I want to put her on."

"You're too short," I said to him and then to my dad, "He's too short."

My dad said, "Let Lizzie do it, Booker. Next year you can do it."

I couldn't believe it. For once someone was on my side.

Holding the angel lightly under the wings, I walked up the stairs to our loft, reached over the railing, and set her gently down onto the top of the tree.

"I swear," said my dad, "if that tree had a voice it would be singing Christmas carols right now."

"It's a perfect tree and a perfect symbol of Christmas," said my mother.

"How about we have some eggnog?" my dad said.

"Great," said my mom.

We all started for the kitchen. I was the last one out of the room. Just as I was turning the corner to enter the kitchen I looked back at the tree.

There it was, a normal beautiful-looking Christmas tree, and then I thought I saw something. It could've been a flash of light or something moving quickly in the branches.

Maybe a bulb burnt out. Maybe there is a bird in the tree, I thought. Maybe I'm going crazy.

My dad stuck his head around the corner and said, "Lizzie."

I jumped sixty feet in the air.

"Don't scare me like that," I said.

"Sorry," he said, "are you coming?"

"Yes," I said, "and Dad? I think I need my eyes checked."

"How many fingers do I have up?" he asked.

"Twenty-seven," I answered.

"Your eyes are fine," he said.

We went into the kitchen and had eggnog. It took my mother a month to find the nutmeg.

I said, "It already has nutmeg in it, mother."

It was right out of the carton, and I could read the ingredients.

"Besides," I said, "this isn't eggnog. It doesn't have any eggs in it. It's fake."

"I just want it to look pretty," said my mom.

"Fine," I said, "whatever."

My mother finally found the nutmeg. Then she had to find the little thing that grinds it. That took forever.

Then she had to find the Christmas mugs we got last year for a present. By the time she gave us each fake eggnog out of the stupid carton, with real nutmeg sprinkled on top, I wasn't even thirsty. However, I didn't say a word.

This part was great.

My dad said, "Cheers," and started clinking cups with everybody.

He clinked with me and then with my mom. He then clinked with Booger. Stupid Booger clinked so hard he dumped his eggnog all over himself and the floor.

Of course he didn't get in trouble. I did.

I swear to you all I said was, "Merry Christmas, moron."

❅ 8 ❅

That night I had a dream. I was standing in front of the Christmas tree and I was having a weird conversation with the angel on top of the tree. There seemed to be a lot of wind in the room, I mean, *a lot*.

In fact, the wind was blowing so hard that I could barely hear the angel. My nightgown was blowing all over the place, and I thought it was a miracle that the decorations weren't blown off the tree.

I could just sort of hear the angel say, "Don't be afraid."

I thought, How original. Angels always say that.

I cupped my hands to my mouth to shout through them. "I can barely hear you," I said.

The angel said again, "Don't be afraid."

I said, "I heard that part."

Then the angel said it again. "Don't be afraid."

I had the feeling she was going to tell me what not to be afraid of, but suddenly she got very bright like she was radioactive or something. I had to put my hands over my eyes because she was so bright, and then she vanished and the wind stopped.

The next morning at breakfast I asked my dad why angels would say, "Don't be afraid."

He said it was probably because when people saw them they went into shock because they're not something you see every day. He then asked me what I thought.

"I don't know," I said, "maybe they think we're a bunch of chickens and we should be more brave."

"Good answer," said my dad. "Next time you talk to an angel ask him and find out."

"Very funny," I said.

My mom said, "Phil, you're going to be late for work."

"Poor Dad," I said, "has to go to work while we're on vacation."

"Poor Dad is right," he said, giving me a hug. "I'll meet you at Michael's for lunch at noon sharp."

He said "sharp" because my mother is always late. We were going shopping and then meeting my dad for lunch. My mom had the week off.

"How come you're off and Dad isn't?" asked Booger.

"Because," she answered, "I have a nice boss and I don't have my Christmas shopping done. So let's get a move on."

We hurried and got dressed and went to the mall. It was the day before Christmas Eve, and all the way in the car my mom kept saying that the mall was going to be packed. She was right. It took us forever to find a place to park, and then we were so far away I suggested that we call a taxi to take us to the door.

"Don't start in, Elizabeth," my mother said.

"Mother," I said, "I just don't understand . . ."

"You just don't know when to quit, do you?" she said.

I didn't want to be there. The only reason I went was to go out to lunch. I knew before we left that I was going to be bored out of my mind following my mother around with her list sixty miles long and having her ask me several hundred times where Booger was. I prefer to shop from catalogs.

"Where's Booker?" my mother asked.

I said, "Why don't you put a leash on him?"

"Lizzie," she said, "the way you talk about him people would think you don't like him."

"I don't," I said.

"I hope Santa is listening right this minute," she said.

"Sorry," I said.

This is another part of Christmas I don't understand. Before Christmas all parents act like you're not going to get any presents if you don't act perfect. I feel like I have to play along with it for some reason.

Every year I act the same. I'm never perfect and I still get presents. The only thing I can figure out is that it must make them feel good to say it.

I had just been sent to go find Booger for the seventeen hundredth time when I saw him; not Booger, but Ralph.

Over by a Christmas tree in the middle of Logan's Department Store was Ralph, the magic Christmas tree man. I don't know what got into me. I mean, I stay away from strangers. He is strange for sure.

I walked up to him and said, "Are you Ralph?"

"Yes," he said, "I sold you your Christmas tree. How do you like it?"

I didn't say anything for a minute.

Then I asked, "Is there something wrong with our tree?"

"What do you mean?" he said.

"I don't know," I said. "I just wonder if there's something in it."

He laughed. "What would be in your tree?"

Then he turned and touched one of the store's Christmas trees. I couldn't tell exactly what he was doing, but it looked like he was putting something on it or taking something off. I thought for a minute he might be shoplifting.

Then he looked right at me. He wasn't laughing now. He looked serious. He said, "Lizzie, I need to tell you . . ."

Just then my mother came up behind me and touched my shoulder and scared the living daylights out of me.

"Where's Booker?" she said.

When I calmed down I said, "Look who's here."

"Who?" said my mother.

"Ralph," I said turning toward him, but where he'd been standing, there was now a lady with a stupid hat on looking at ornaments on the tree.

"He was just here," I said.

"Booker?" asked my mother.

"No, you know, Ralph, the Christmas tree man."

"Really," said my mother raising her eyebrows, "and you talked to him?"

"Sort of," I said.

"Honey," she said, "you know you shouldn't talk to strangers."

"Mom, he isn't a real stranger, and it was no big deal."

"It's a big deal to me," said my mother.

Booger came out from behind the tree.

"There you are," said my mother.

"Look at this," he said. "Can I buy it?"

It was a Christmas ornament, sort of. It was so ugly you wouldn't want to call it an ornament.

It was just the sort of thing Booger would have picked out.

"It's a dancing man," said Booger.

"It's ugly," I said.

I looked at it closer.

"Too weird, Mom," I said. "Don't buy it."

It was a man with his arms and legs in the air like he was dancing. There was something familiar about it.

"Mom," said Booger, "can't I have it?"

"It is on sale. It's kind of cute. Oh, why not?" she said.

"You give him everything he wants," I said.

She ignored me. She bought it. I couldn't believe it.

In the car, I asked Booger if I could look at it again, but he said he was looking at it.

"Well," I said, "when you're through, could I look at it?"

"No," he said.

My mom finally told him to let me see it.

I held it in my hand and it hit me why I didn't like it. There was something familiar about it, all right. It looked like Ralph. It looked like strange Ralph dancing his legs off.

❄ 9 ❄

When we drove into the driveway I told my mom, "Something is going to happen."

"What do you mean?" she asked. "Are you getting sick?"

I was kind of cranky and said, "If I knew, I would have told you, and I'm not getting sick."

She looked at me a minute like she was going to say something, but then she took a deep breath and didn't. She got out of the car and walked toward the house. I caught up with her.

I was going to say "I'm sorry, Mom," but I just couldn't make myself do it.

"Lizzie, Christmas seems to bring out the best and the worst in people," she said. "Please try to concentrate on the best."

We walked into the door of the house and I looked at the Christmas tree. I thought it shivered when I looked at it. It didn't shake or move its branches like a breeze had hit it. It shivered as if it were cold or afraid. It kind of gave me the creeps.

I thought, It knows something is going to happen, too.

My mom didn't see it, or if she did, she sure didn't say anything.

She said, "Oh, Booker, get the new ornament and put it on."

She then went into her bedroom to dump her sacks. Booker and I followed her in. She handed Booker the sack with the ornament in it. The ornament was all wrapped up like someone thought it could break.

I thought, We should be so lucky.

Booger took it out of the paper and went down the hall to put it on the tree. I followed him.

My mother yelled after me, "Lizzie, don't do anything."

I didn't have to do anything. Booger put the ornament on one of the lower branches because they were the ones he could reach.

I said, "You realize it won't stay there."

He said, "I'll tell Mom if you move it."

"I won't have to move it, you idiot."

"What do you mean?" he asked.

"Let's just go into the other room for a second and see what happens," I answered.

We went into the kitchen and then came right back out. The ornament was now way up by the angel.

My mom walked into the room. "Perfect place for him, Booker, but how did you reach that high?"

I said, "You don't want to know, Mom."

"Lizzie," she said.

Booker started to tell her what had happened, which I knew she wouldn't believe anyway. Just then my dad walked through the door.

"Hi, I'm home," he said.

"You certainly are," said my mom.

"What's to eat?" he said.

"Whatever you fix," said my mother.

"Don't you mean whatever *we* fix?" he said.

"It's a date," my mom said. "Better yet, it's a family affair. Booker, Liz, let's head for the kitchen."

"This is a mistake," I said.

"C'mon, Lizzie," my mom said, "go for the best not the worst, remember?"

Booger came in the room and he was picking his nose. I looked at my mother.

"He has to wash his hands or I'm not eating."

"We'll all wash our hands," she said, "and then we'll all cook up a storm."

We washed our hands and then we were in the kitchen. We'd voted and decided to have waffles for dinner. We know they're for breakfast, but they are practically everyone's favorite, and we never have time to make them in the morning. Besides they're sort of fast.

My job was to mix up the batter for the waffles.

Booger was supposed to set the table. Of course, he forgot to give me any silverware.

"I didn't get a fork or a knife," I said when we sat down at the table.

"I gave you one," said Booger.

"What a little liar," I said.

"Lizzie," said my mother, "why don't you just get up and get what you need."

"If I had set the table, you would've made me go get it for him," I said.

As I got up I accidentally bumped dumbhead's chair. How was I supposed to know he was going to take a huge bite just then and poke his big fat upper lip with his fork? Served him right for being such a pig.

"Lizzie," said my mom, "that's it. As soon as you're done clearing the table after dinner, you're to go to bed."

"Not fair," I said. "I didn't do anything. It was an accident."

"There are way too many accidents in this house," said my mother. "Now hurry up and get your silverware. Sit down and eat your dinner and then get ready for bed."

"Why are you always on his side?" I asked.

My dad said, "Lizzie, that's enough. This discussion is over."

I thought, but didn't say, I wish I was someplace else, far away from my stupid mother and my stupid brother.

My mother was trying to be cheery. She was talking about the crazy people at the shopping mall. She said she was going to get her Christmas shopping done in June next year.

I was going to tell her that she says that every year, but I had decided I was through talking.

After dinner I cleared the table. I then took a bath. I refused to wash my hair. I was just waiting for them to say something about it, but they didn't, so I went to bed.

I was reading and my mom came in and turned off the light.

"With lights out," she said.

"That is so unfair," I said. "I should be able to read."

"Not when you treat people badly," she said.

"Great," I said. "I'm not going to change, so you might as well put me to bed for the rest of my life. I guess I'll never read again."

"Good night Lizzie," said my mom.

I showed her. I fell asleep within ten minutes.

❄ **10** ❄

I don't know how long I had slept but I know this: I woke up and I was dying of thirst. I got up and went down the hall. I passed my parents' bedroom. I could see my dad sleeping. I passed Booger's room and he was snoring.

"Isn't that a pretty sound," I said.

I wondered where my mom was.

She probably stayed up late to wrap presents, I thought.

Without turning on the lights I went into the kitchen and got a drink. I saw the living room lights were on. I could see them shining underneath the door.

I figured I should at least peek in and see who was in there. I knew it was my mom. I was pretty sure it was my mom, but just in case I was still in trouble, or in case it was a burglar, I opened the door just a crack. It was my mom.

I could only see her back. She was standing in

front of the Christmas tree. She looked like a statue or something.

I opened the door a little wider and said, "Mom?"

I said it real quiet because I didn't want to scare her.

She didn't hear me.

"Mom?" I said again, a little louder.

Then I saw the tree flash like it did before, or whatever that thing is.

I came into the room and said, "Mom," in a normal voice.

She didn't turn around. In fact, she started walking right up to the tree. I moved toward her.

"Mother," I said, "can't you hear me calling you?"

If she could she was ignoring me. She was right up with her body against the tree now. I came up behind her and reached out to touch her.

I felt a soft wind coming from the tree. The branches were moving.

"Mom, this isn't funny," I said.

Then my mother pushed aside two of the branches and she walked into the tree. It was totally weird. I mean she was gone. She had walked into the middle of the tree and she was gone.

I went around to the back of the tree to look for her. I felt totally stupid doing it, too. She wasn't there. I was kind of in shock for a second.

I yelled for her.

"Mom! Get out of the Christmas tree!"

I was getting a little freaked out.

I started pulling branches open and knocked off a bunch of ornaments. She wasn't in there.

I said to myself, "Lizzie, don't panic. Go get Dad."

I flew down the hall into my parents' bedroom.

"Dad, wake up," I yelled. "Mom is inside the Christmas tree."

He wouldn't wake up. At first I thought he was dead, but he was breathing. I shook him like crazy. He just wouldn't wake up.

I was getting scared. I guess I was also getting desperate. I went into Booger's room.

"Booger," I said, shaking him, "get up. Mom is in trouble."

Booger wouldn't move.

I'm dreaming, I thought. I'm not going to panic. I'm going to go lie down on my bed and wake myself up. Very simple.

I went into my room, laid down on my bed, and pinched my thigh. It hurt like crazy and I didn't wake up. I had to try something else.

I went over to my bulletin board and got a pin. I poked my left thumb with it. It hurt like the dickens and it bled.

I said, "You don't bleed in dreams."

I knew I must be awake. This was really happening. I went back into my dad's room.

I said, "This is going to hurt me more than it's going to hurt you," which was real stupid because it wasn't going to hurt me a bit. I slugged him big-time in the arm. He didn't even budge.

I could've done it to Booger but I didn't. I think everyone should know that.

I said, "I'm not going to panic. What am I going to do?"

I thought I could call 911, but I didn't know what to say.

"Hi, this is Lizzie, and my mother just walked into our Christmas tree, and I can't get her out, and my dad and brother won't wake up."

They'd think I was a crazy person.

Maybe I am a crazy person, I thought.

Just then I could hear more wind in the living room. It sounded like someone had opened a door and left it open. The wind was coming through the house.

Quickly I put on the clothes I had left on my floor. I was glad I left them on the floor instead of putting them away. Having your clothes handy certainly makes it a lot faster getting dressed in an emergency.

I hopped down the hall still tying my shoes.

I asked myself, "Lizzie, what are you doing? You are crazy. Why did you get dressed?"

Then I knew. I was going to get my mom out of that tree.

I'll go to the garage and get the ax and chop her out, I thought.

Then I realized I couldn't see her to chop her out.

I went into the living room. I thought of that dumb joke.

You know the one that goes, "If everyone is going to die, where's the safest place in the house?"

The answer is, "The living room."

I looked around. There were no doors or windows open. There didn't seem to be any wind. I went over to the tree.

I pulled some more branches apart and tried to see inside. I could almost see the trunk.

"This thing is so thick," I said, "it's ridiculous."

I stepped back a minute.

"Mom, are you in there?" I asked.

I thought I heard a voice. It wasn't my mom's voice, but it sounded like someone I knew. I just couldn't remember whose voice it was.

Then I saw a flash of light at the center of the tree. I felt the light winds. I thought I could see the middle of the tree open up.

I pulled open the branches. This time the tree was opening up.

"Here goes nothing," I said as I lifted my foot to step inside.

✳ **11** ✳

W ait," I said, "what am I doing? I can't get her back. I don't know where she is and I don't know where I am."

I was somewhere in the tree. I had pitch in my hair.

Great, I thought, now, I really need to wash it.

I had branches in my eyes and in my ears. I had them in my ribs. I was glad I had my shoes on. I was stepping on branches with every step. I was in a pitchy, thick Christmas tree jungle.

"This is stupid," I said. "I'm turning around."

I think I turned around about eight times. I couldn't tell which was the direction back to the living room.

"Great," I said, "I'm lost in my own Christmas tree."

Then I saw a light up ahead. It wasn't that flashing business. It looked like regular light. I hoped it was the lights in our living room.

I kept pushing onward toward it. Something flew in my face. It was a bird.

So there *was* a bird in this tree, I thought.

However, I started to think it wasn't just one tree. I reached a trunk and went around it. Then I reached another, and another, and another. Unless I was going in real tight circles, I wasn't traveling through just one tree. I was going through a whole forest.

"Mom," I whispered, "are you in here?"

I didn't hear anything except the brush of the limbs against me.

I looked up. I couldn't trust my eyes. I thought I saw blue sky in my living room.

I closed my eyes to keep them from getting poked out and pushed my way through the final branches. Suddenly, I was out in the open. I wasn't in my living room.

"What is this place?" I said.

I was glad no one answered me but I still would've liked to have known.

I looked down at my pants and shirt. I had pitch and pollen and dust all over me.

I thought, My mom's going to kill me if I ever find her or if anyone ever finds me.

I looked around. I was in the country — I knew that. I couldn't see any freeways or cities or roads. It looked like spring or early summer.

There were mountains not too far away. I was

in a sort of a clearing. There was a stream just a few yards from me.

I turned around and there was a dense forest behind me. I was all alone. At least I thought I was all alone.

I saw a deer in the distance. There were birds. I even saw a rabbit. I didn't see any people.

I tried yelling, "Mom!" but I didn't get an answer.

I next tried, "Anyone home?" and I heard an echo far away: "Home, home, home, home."

Well, with no one to talk to, I had to talk to myself.

"Now what are you going to do?" I asked.

I answered, "Go back."

I looked at the forest behind me. It was too thick. I could be lost for days, maybe years.

I said, "I don't think that's a good idea."

I answered myself, "*I* don't think that's a good idea, either."

I got this fantastic idea. I was thinking about all the books I'd read, where you go to like a different world, and the animals can talk and they'll help you.

I went toward the deer and said, "Can you talk?"

He ran away.

I yelled at the bunny, "Do you speak English?"

He hopped into the forest.

That was a blowout. Then I remembered that

I read somewhere or someone had told me that when you're lost and there's a stream, you should follow it down. I wasn't really lost. I just didn't know where I was. I figured my mother was lost and she probably followed the stream. Maybe she had been the one that had told me that.

I started following the stream. I hiked quite a while. The place was really pleasant. It was daylight.

"Wasn't it nighttime back in my living room?" I asked myself.

I kept walking.

"I wonder where this place is?" I said.

There wasn't any litter. There were no campgrounds. There weren't any mosquitoes. It was weird. The place was, like, too perfect.

Then I saw a person. He was quite a ways away, but I could see a man. He was jumping around or something.

I wondered if he was dangerous. I wondered if I had any choice in the matter. I wondered what I was doing.

I walked slowly toward him. As I got closer I realized he wasn't jumping. He was dancing. He was singing and dancing. He couldn't sing very well, and if you ask me, he didn't dance so hot either, but that's what he was doing.

"Excuse me," I said, "do you know what this place is?"

The man stopped dancing and looked at me. I

nearly had a heart attack. It was Ralph, the magic Christmas tree man.

"What are you doing here?" I asked.

"I suppose I could ask you the same thing," he replied.

"I'm looking for my mom," I said.

"I'm waiting for someone," he said.

"How did you get here?" I asked.

"You tell first," he said.

"I walked through our Christmas tree," I said.

"Really?" he said.

"Yes, really, and you sold it to us and you knew it would do this."

"I had a feeling . . ." he said.

"How did you get here?" I asked.

"Well," he said, "I come here different ways. I have come through a Christmas tree before."

"Have you seen my mother?"

"No," said Ralph. "You're sure she's here?"

I said, "She came through the tree before I did."

He looked worried.

"What's wrong?" I said.

"I hope nothing," he said.

❄ **12** ❄

Y ou're inside," said Ralph.
I had asked him again where I was.

"It's kind of hard to explain," he said.

"I believe it," I said.

"We're inside," he said.

"You already told me that," I said. "We're inside. I got that part. What are we inside of?"

"We're not on Earth exactly," said Ralph, "but we're not that far from it."

"Just a Christmas tree away?" I said.

Ralph thought that was real funny. I didn't trust this guy as far as you could throw him. I guarantee that wouldn't be very far.

"Honest," he said, "that's the truth."

"How are we inside?" I asked. "Inside of the tree?"

Ralph said, "Think of it this way. Remember a cold, windy, dark night when you were outside. Where did you want to go?"

"Inside the house," I said, "where it is safe and warm and not dark."

"Exactly," said Ralph. "Now think of your living room as being outside, the Christmas tree being a door, and this" — he spread his arms — "is inside where it is safe and warm."

"Hey," I said, sort of getting it.

He smiled this weak smile at me.

"Are you making this up?" I asked.

"Yeah," he answered, "but it's the truth. I don't know how else to describe it."

I didn't know whether to believe him or not.

"Okay," I said, "so where's my mom?"

"I don't know for sure," said Ralph.

"So how do I find out?" I said.

He said, "I've got a friend. She'll know."

"Where is she?" I asked.

"Who?" he said.

"Your friend," I said.

"She's coming," he said. "She told me she was coming."

Just then there was a huge explosion. I looked up in the sky. That's the direction the noise was coming from.

Ralph said, "Oh, no!"

I started to say, "Oh, no, what?" but he interrupted me.

"How good a dancer are you?" he yelled at me.

"Excuse me?" I said.

"There's no time," he said.

He grabbed both of my wrists.

"Hang on, Lizzie," he said, "this could get a little rough."

"No way," I said and I tried to break loose.

I heard another explosion. I looked back up in the sky. There was a black blob of something up there, and it was heading our way.

"What is that?" I said.

"Start dancing or you're going to find out quicker than you want to," said Ralph.

He started dancing. Well, he was still mostly jumping around, and the way he was going he was jerking me all over the place. I tried to keep up with him so I wouldn't fall down. Then he started spinning us in circles.

For a minute it felt like I wasn't touching the ground.

I thought, Great, a crazy man is getting me dizzy and pulling my arms out of my sockets. Wait until I tell the school counselor this one.

Everything was swirling and I was feeling kind of sick.

"Ralph," I said, "Slow down."

"Hang on," he said.

He was hanging onto my wrists so tight I didn't have to think about hanging on, but for some reason I thought I should. I grabbed both his wrists and then I couldn't see anything but blurring light. I really did think we were flying, but I couldn't see the ground to tell.

I thought, They don't teach you this one in dance class.

Just then I felt something awful grab me. It wasn't like fingers. It was more like a huge vacuum cleaner going after my feet and then my legs. It felt wet and cold and it was pulling on me.

I was screaming but I was only screaming in my head. My mouth couldn't make any sounds. Then, whatever it was got inside me.

It was going up my body inside me. It was in my head. It was telling me to let go. It was in my hands, my fingers. It was prying my fingers loose.

"Don't let me go," I tried to say to Ralph.

That was all I remember and then I was waking up. My head was in a woman's lap and she was singing to me. It was the most amazing song I'd ever listened to.

It wasn't like rock 'n roll or classical music. It wasn't like any music I'd ever heard. It was almost better than music.

I looked up into this woman's face. She was the most beautiful woman I'd ever seen. It was like she was a hundred times prettier than any model you've ever seen. I was close enough to her to tell, and I can tell you this, she didn't have a bit of makeup on. She was totally natural.

Out of her mouth came hundreds of sounds, and it was like they were all playing at once. She seemed to be her own personal karaoke machine.

I mean, she was singing and accompanying herself at the same time.

The only thing I could think was, Amazing.

I still kind of thought I was going to puke. I didn't want to do it in her lap so I got up. I was incredibly dizzy.

"Don't hurry," she said.

Ralph was laughing.

"And what is so dang funny?" I asked.

It would not have bothered me in the least to barf on him.

"I'm sorry," he said. "Are you feeling any better?"

I rubbed my wrists.

"Yes," I said, "but no thanks to you."

Ralph was laughing again.

"What's the joke this time?" I said.

"Not a thing," said Ralph. "I'm just thinking how wild this is for you."

"*Strange* is the word for it," I said.

I looked around. The stream, the mountains, the forest were all gone. Now, we were next to a lake with giant cliffs on the opposite side.

"Where are we now?" I asked. "And if you say inside, I'm going to scream."

The woman stood up. I swear that she was at least seven feet tall. She was gorgeous and she was seven feet tall. She was wearing a white — I don't know what to call it, because it wasn't a dress or a robe or a coat. It was this amazing beautiful garment, and when it moved you could see rainbows of pastel colors wash through it.

"Who are you?" I asked.

"Oh, I'm sorry," said Ralph. "This is Gloria, the friend I was telling you about. Gloria, this is Lizzie."

"Pleased to meet you," I said.

"Don't be afraid," said Gloria.

"Huh?" I said.

❄ 13 ❄

Do we have to start right now?" asked Gloria. "Can't we give her some time at least to rest?"

"You saw what just happened," said Ralph.

Gloria sighed and then said, "She's so young."

"But she's strong," said Ralph.

I said, "I got the Presidential Award for Fitness for the last two years."

Ralph laughed.

"You're strong in many ways," he said.

I didn't particularly like the way he said that.

"Where's my mom?" I asked.

"Don't be afraid," Gloria said.

"I'm not," I said.

I just stood there for a minute. I don't know why, but I couldn't help it. I just totally cracked up. It must have been the stress. I laughed hysterically.

I finally stopped.

"Sorry," I said to Gloria. "I don't know why I

was laughing. I wasn't laughing at you, really."

"No offense taken," said Gloria.

I thought, This woman could be the nicest person I have ever met.

I asked Gloria again, "Where is my mom? Do you know?"

"She's temporarily lost," said Gloria.

"But we know where she's lost," said Ralph.

"If you know where she is, she's not lost," I said.

"We don't know where she is exactly," said Gloria. "We know where she is lost."

"I'm totally confused. Could you just show me where she is so I can go get her?" I asked.

"We will," said Ralph, "but getting her is not that simple."

Gloria said, "We'll try to help."

I said, "Don't talk to me about help. I couldn't wake up my dad, and I didn't call the police because I didn't know what on earth to say."

"Good help is hard to find," said Ralph, laughing.

I rolled my eyes at Gloria.

She said, "Don't mind him. He means well."

I thought, He's still strange.

I trusted Gloria though. It wasn't just because she was nice and pretty. There was something else about her that made me feel like I'd known her a long time. She reminded me of someone. I couldn't figure out who.

Ralph said, "Lizzie, do you remember something pulling on you when we were dancing?"

It all came back to me. A shiver went up my spine just thinking about it.

I started to say, "What was that?"

Then I realized what had happened.

"That thing got my mom, didn't it?"

Neither Gloria nor Ralph said anything.

Okay, I admit it, I was a little scared.

Gloria said, "Don't be afraid."

I said, "If you'd stop saying that, I wouldn't be afraid."

"Sorry," said Gloria, "it's just a habit."

We all three looked at each other.

"What is that thing that has my mom? I think I should know," I said.

"Okay," said Ralph, taking a deep breath, "I'm just going to lay all the cards on the table."

Gloria cleared her throat as if she were going to say something, but she didn't.

Ralph continued, "This is what we know about it. We know it's very dark and it's very confusing. We don't know what it is or why it is here."

"I don't mean to be impolite," I said, "but it doesn't sound like you know very much."

"Sorry," said Gloria.

"Has it always been here?" I asked.

"No," said Gloria.

"How did it get here?" I asked.

"It was brought in," said Ralph.

"Why would someone want to bring it in?" I asked. "That would be totally stupid."

Gloria half smiled and raised her eyebrows.

"It's a mystery," said Ralph. "I doubt we'll ever understand it fully."

"I guess we should go ahead," said Gloria.

"To go get my mom?" I said, and my voice sort of cracked.

"No," said Ralph. "First we have to show you where she is."

I said, "The place where she's lost, but not lost, because we know where she's lost."

"Uh-huh," said Ralph.

"Will going there be dangerous?" I asked.

"Yes," said Gloria, "but we'll be with you."

"Are you ready?" said Ralph.

"Do I have a choice?" I asked.

"Always," said Gloria. "You always have a choice."

Everything seemed kind of tense.

"Oh, I'm ready," I said, and then I thought I was going to be sick.

"Which direction is it?" I asked.

Ralph replied, "Oh, we'll dance there. You're getting good at the steps."

I asked Gloria, "I got the distinct impression that I flew here. Is that true?"

"It's truly more like dancing. Flying is something else again," answered Gloria.

"I mean, I was by this stream and then Ralph

was jerking me around, pulling my arms out of my sockets, and I ended up here, and I don't think we could've danced this far."

"Strange as it seems . . ." said Ralph.

I said, "I've never danced before starting in one place and ending in a completely different place."

"You just didn't know the right steps," said Ralph.

"I guess if I got here originally by walking through my Christmas tree, anything is possible."

"Would you like to try dancing with me?" asked Gloria.

How could I refuse?

Gloria grabbed one hand, Ralph the other, and they said together, "Let's dance!"

❋ 14 ❋

Everything started whirling.

I thought, I hope I don't get carsick, or air-sick, or I guess dance-sick.

With Gloria or maybe because I had experience it seemed like the ride was a lot smoother. Also, that thing wasn't trying to get me. That made a huge difference.

We stopped. We were in a desert with white fog clear up to our knees. I turned to look around.

"What in the world is that?" I asked.

Right in front of us was a huge black wall that went up into the sky as far as you could see.

"That is where your mother is," said Gloria.

"She's inside," said Ralph.

To say I was impressed was putting it mildly.

"Just look at it a minute," said Gloria. "Don't touch it. It doesn't know we're here yet."

"Don't worry," I said.

I thought of my mother being in there and I got kind of sad.

"It's a little scary, isn't it?" I said to Gloria.

She smiled at me and touched my hair.

I looked at the dark wall. It had looked solid before but now it was quivering. It looked like thick, oily, black wiggling Jell-O.

"It knows we're here," said Gloria.

"Quick, grab my hand," said Ralph.

I grabbed both of their hands and started jumping up and down like crazy. I had no idea how to dance out of there but I was giving it all I had.

We must have danced even faster than the times before because it seemed like we were just in the desert and then we were back by the lake.

I must have looked pretty serious because Ralph said to me, "It isn't that bad, kid."

I said, "Your mom isn't in there."

He said, "I didn't know you cared about your mom that much. I thought you were always in trouble."

That really ticked me off.

"How would you know?" I asked. "I just so happen to love my mother very much. It is true that she doesn't always treat me fairly, but she's still my mother."

"Oh," said Ralph.

I could've just slugged him right there and then.

"Don't be mad at Ralph," said Gloria. "He's helping you not be afraid. It seems to love it when we're afraid."

"Know any jokes?" said Ralph.

"What are you talking about?" I asked.

Gloria said, "It also is very serious, but we must remember not to take it too seriously."

"What's the point here?" I asked. "I feel like you're playing games with me."

Gloria replied, "We're just trying to get you ready to go in and get your mother. That is what you want to do, isn't it?"

"Absolutely," I said. "Just give it to me straight."

Gloria put both her hands on my shoulders, bent down, and looked me in the eyes. "Remember this one thing. Your weaknesses are also your strengths."

Gloria shivered. "I'm sorry," she said. "It's time. We have to hurry. Your mother can't hold on much longer."

"Which weaknesses?" I asked. "I have several."

"We've got to go," said Ralph, springing to his feet.

I stood up and took a gulp of air. I think I was going to say that I needed a little more preparation, that I didn't completely understand the plan. However, before I could say a word they had grabbed my hands again and in a flash we were back at the edge of whatever that thing was.

I looked at it and it quivered.

"It knows I'm here," I said.

It looked like it had gotten darker. I don't know how black can be darker, but it was.

I thought, You can't really expect me to go into that thing. Real little girls do not go walking into very dark mean places whether they are looking for their mothers or not.

"Be brave," said Gloria.

"Okay," I said, "I'm laughing, see?"

I fake laughed.

Ralph said, "Try a little harder."

"How do we get in?" I asked.

Gloria said, "*We* don't. I can't go in."

"You're kidding me," I said. "Why not?"

"Watch," said Gloria. "It will not let me in."

Gloria walked up to the wall. She turned and grabbed her elbow like she was going to bash a door down. Then with all her might she hit it with the side of her body.

I picked her up off the ground.

"It won't let me in," she said.

"Then it won't let me in," I said.

I went over to it. I put my arm out and touched it. It was dreadful.

It felt slimy and cold and wet. The worst thing was, my hand went right through it.

"I guess it will," I said.

I pulled back my arm and turned toward where Ralph was.

"I guess it's just you and me, Ralph," I said, but Ralph was gone.

I knew I couldn't trust that guy.

"Gloria, where did he go?" I turned back to ask Gloria but now she was gone, too.

"Yoo-hoo!" I said. "Anybody home?"

❋ 15 ❋

I screamed as loud as I could, "You can't leave me here!"

No one answered me.

I was just stupid. I yelled for my dad. I even yelled for Booger. I yelled for anyone.

I screamed, "Help!" fifty million times until my throat was sore.

I looked over at the dark wall. It looked smooth and shiny like glass. It acted like it was just waiting for me.

I walked up to it. It was so smooth I could see my reflection in it.

"Nice hair," I said to myself. I wished I had washed it.

I tried to comb it with my fingers.

Then there was like a ripple in the reflection. There was a girl there and she sort of looked like me, but it wasn't me.

I said, "Mom?"

It was. It was the reflection of my mother, but

my mother as a girl my age. I looked in her eyes. She looked lonely and scared, and all I wanted to do was hug her. I reached out to touch her, and the reflection was gone.

"Shoot, Lizzie," I said. "Just go in there and take a look around. Stop being such a big baby."

I'd made up my mind. Sometimes it makes sense to do things without thinking about them that much. It's just like when you jump off a high diving board.

At some point you have to stop thinking about being a chicken and just jump whether you want to or not. I quit thinking and I walked right into the darkest dang thing you can imagine. Immediately I got just a teeny hysterical.

I said, "Lizzie, what have you done?"

I hated the feel of it on my face and for the first few seconds I couldn't see a thing. Then I thought my eyes were getting used to it because I looked down and saw my hands. Then I realized it was because they were glowing.

I glowed in the dark. It was weird. I looked like one of those glow-in-the-dark fish in the pet store with a black light on it. I was fluorescent.

At that point I was feeling pretty cool.

This isn't that scary, I thought.

Then something brushed past me. It was alive or at least it was moving. Then I heard other things moving around me. Even though I could see myself, I couldn't see anything but darkness wherever I looked.

"Who's there?" I said.

At first there was no answer.

I repeated myself, "Who's there?"

Then inside my head I heard a voice and it wasn't mine.

It said, "No one. There is no one here, no one."

✳ **16** ✳

I checked out my hands. I thought they looked a little dimmer.

"Mom?" I called out but there was no answer inside or outside my head.

I was afraid to move. I tried to think of which direction I came in. I couldn't see anything but the stupid dark.

I told myself I couldn't just stand there. I heard something to the right of me so I turned in the other direction and started walking.

I did think, What if I'm walking into the middle of this thing?

Actually, I was more sliding my feet than walking. The ground underneath me felt like sand. It didn't feel solid so I felt like I was losing my balance all the time.

Even though I was still glowing, it wasn't enough to light a very large area. I always felt like I was going to bump into something or hit my head. My eyes were killing me trying to see anything.

I heard more things move around me, or at least I thought I did. The place smelled, too, like wet garbage.

The voice that wasn't mine in my head said, "There's no one there. There's no one here."

I walked at least seven thousand miles and I was starting to get really scared. I was trying not to cry.

I thought, How can I get back out of here?

Then I said out loud, "Where is the light switch?"

The voice answered me and said, "There is no light. The light is gone."

"Get going, Lizzie," I said.

"There's no place to go," said the voice.

"Don't listen to that voice," I told myself.

"There's nothing to listen to," said the voice.

I thought, I'm getting kind of tired.

The voice said, "Rest, there is nowhere to go."

"Who are you?" I yelled.

There wasn't an answer.

"Who is the voice inside my head?" I asked.

It answered, "There is no voice. There is no head."

Suddenly I was very cold. I was colder than being out in winter without a coat. I was colder than sitting in a movie theater with the air-conditioning set below zero.

It was so cold it was making me numb. I couldn't walk anymore. I couldn't think.

"Rest," said the voice. "Lie down and rest. You're not here."

I was so tired. I didn't know where I was. I didn't know who I was.

I have to remember something, I thought.

"There's nothing to remember," said the voice.

"What's my name?" I asked.

"Name for what?" asked the voice.

"I don't remember," I said.

I looked at my hands and I could barely see them. I laid myself down on the ground.

I thought, Maybe I'll just close my eyes and rest for a while.

Why wasn't I afraid?

The voice was silent.

Everything was silent. Everything was dark and silent.

❄ **17** ❄

I thought I was asleep and dreaming. I was thinking I was having one really weird dream. It was about being in the dark and falling asleep and forgetting something.

I almost laughed but then I opened my eyes and I couldn't see anything. I was on the ground in the dark. I was getting depressed.

It was real. It wasn't a dream. I stood up.

"I have to remember something," I said.

The voice said, "There's nothing to remember."

I was starting to remember. I remembered that Gloria had told me something.

"I sort of remember," I said.

"There's nothing to remember," it said.

"Oh, yes there is," I said. "Gloria told me . . ."

"Gloria didn't say anything. There is nothing to remember."

I thought, Gloria said . . .

The voice said, "There is no Gloria."

"Yes, there is," I said, "and I remember what

she said. She said my weaknesses were also my strengths, but I don't know what it means."

The voice was about to make a big mistake.

It said, "You have no weaknesses."

"You're wrong this time for sure. Just ask my mom. She always tells me I don't know when to quit. If that isn't a weakness I don't know what it is."

The voice was silent.

"That's it," I shrieked. "That isn't my weakness! It may look like it but it's not. It's my strength! I don't know when to quit."

The voice said, "There's nothing to quit."

"Wrong," I said. "Quit you!"

I started moving again.

I told the voice, "Talk all you want. I'm not listening. I don't have to."

The voice was eerily silent.

I kept walking and I kept bumping into things.

"Sorry," I said every time it happened but no one answered back.

Then I saw someone or something faintly glowing ahead. I moved toward it cautiously. I reached down and touched it.

"Mom?" I said.

She didn't act like she heard me. She didn't even seem to feel it when I touched her. She was limp.

I thought, I came all this way, I found my mom, and now we'll never get out. I can't drag her.

The voice was back.

"There's no place to go," it said.

"That's it," I said, "I've *had* it."

I yelled at my mother. I've yelled at my mother before, but this time I knew she wouldn't ground me for it.

"C'mon, Mom," I said, pulling on her arm. "We've got to get out of here."

"Lizzie," she said, "where are you?"

She sounded like she'd just woken up.

"Mom," I said, "I'm right here."

She looked at me.

"Lizzie," she said, "where are we?"

"Mom," I said, "it's a long story. I'm glad to see you, but we've got to get out of here as fast as possible. Can you get up?"

"I think so," she said.

She started to get up but then she sat down.

"Mom," I said, "what are you doing? Get up."

She said, "I thought you told me to sit down and rest."

"Wrong, Mom," I said. "That's the voice telling you that, and you have to ignore it. It makes you forget what you're doing."

"Forget what?" she asked.

I don't know what came over me but I got all weird.

I said, "Mom, it will make you forget how much I love you, no matter what."

"Oh, honey," she said and she hugged me.

She was better. She stood up.

I said, "She walks. She talks. She's almost human!"

My mother laughed.

"Mom," I said, "we've got to get to some light."

"Light?" she said, acting kind of spacey.

"Yes, Mom, light," I said. "Look around. Do you see any?"

She looked all around us. It was pitch-black wherever you looked. She then pulled herself up straight and tall.

"Yes, sirree," she said, "we should find some light."

I said, "Mom, we have to get out of here as soon as possible."

"Sounds like a good plan," she said. "Do you know which way to go?"

I sort of lied and said, "Yes."

I got her to run for a little while. I couldn't tell how far or how long. Things just don't make sense in the dark. I did notice I was starting to breathe a little heavy. We switched to jogging.

"It tries to confuse you," I said.

"What does?" my mother asked.

She was panting like crazy. My mom isn't in very good shape.

"Mom," I yelled, "you can't slow down."

She was walking now, holding her side, and I could tell she was ready to stop.

She said, "I just have to rest a minute. I'm not

used to running like this. Just let me rest a minute. I'm so tired. Aren't you tired?"

"Mom," I said, "you can't do this. We have to keep moving."

"I can't," she said, and she stopped right there.

point to winning like this. I didn't care anymore.

"Mom," I said, "you've got to try. We have to keep moving."

I started, and then I stopped.

❄ **18** ❄

I knew we were in big trouble. I tried pulling her. I tried pushing her, but it was no good.

"So tired," she said, sounding like she was repeating it to someone.

I knew she had the voice in her head. I just knew it.

"Light," I yelled in her ear, "you've got to think about getting back out into the light."

She looked at me like I was from the moon. I didn't know what I was going to do.

"Help!" I yelled.

Of course there was no answer. I watched my mom get visibly dimmer. It was like she was a house and someone was going through her turning off all the lights.

Then I felt a strong pull like super gravity. Whatever this thing was, it was pulling on us. It was holding onto us like huge weights. I couldn't even think of moving.

It felt like it was dragging us on a carpet. We were being pulled deeper, back into the dark. I heard the voice.

"Rest," it said, "there is no light."

"Did you tell me to rest?" asked my mom.

"No," I answered, getting really mad at her, "and we're not giving up."

I felt it let go for just a second. Was it because I got mad at my mom or was it because I said I wasn't giving up? I didn't have time to think about it.

I looked for some place to go. I couldn't see anything but stupid darkness. It didn't take long for the voice to come back.

It said, "There's nothing to see."

I was really mad now. I yelled so loud I could have knocked a building down with my voice.

"Shut up!"

If I'd done that at school, I would have been in detention for a month.

Right then two things happened. First, it felt like the darkness let go again. Then, just about ten feet away, it was like someone cut a hole in a blanket and light was pouring through.

A glowing arm was reaching out to us. I got my mother moving toward it.

"See, Mom," I yelled, acting like a maniac, "see the light?"

"Yeah," she said, "I see it."

We were moving again. I've never been so happy in my life. A voice came through the rip. It was that creep Ralph.

"C'mon," he said, "get out of there."

Then the hurricane hit. We were being attacked full force. It was doing its vacuum cleaner number. It was awful. I couldn't even breathe.

I can't make it, I thought.

"Rest," said the voice.

"Hang on," yelled Ralph.

My mom was trying to pry my hands off hers. I was trying to stop her.

"No, Mom," I said, crying like a big baby, "I love you. Please don't let go. We have to get out of here."

She stopped. We started moving forward.

"Ralph," I hollered, "don't leave. We're going to make it."

I could feel the drag on us loosening. I reached for Ralph's hand. Suddenly we were there. He pulled us through.

Gloria had been holding onto Ralph so when we popped out we all ended up on the ground on top of her.

"Don't be afraid," she said.

✳ **19** ✳

Y ou did it!" said Ralph.
  Gloria hugged me.

"Where did you go?" I said to Ralph.

"You didn't need my help till the end," he said.

"Oh, *really*?" I said.

Then I remembered the dark thing. I looked behind me to check on it. Yes, I was still a little jumpy. It wasn't there.

"Where'd it go?" I spat out.

"It's gone," said Gloria. "For now."

My mom looked cranky.

"Where am I?" she asked. "I'm very confused. Who are you people? Where am I?"

"Mom," I replied, introducing them, "you know Ralph. He's the one who sold us that maniac Christmas tree, and this is my friend Gloria."

"Pleased to meet you," she said, adding, "beautiful gown," to Gloria. "Where did you say I was?" my mom asked.

We were back by the stream where I first came inside.

"We didn't," said Ralph, "but you're on your way home now."

"Somehow," she said, "I thought that would be the sort of answer I'd get."

"Are you going to dance us home?" I asked.

My mother looked at me like I was nuts.

"Sorry," said Gloria.

"You'll have to do it the hard way," said Ralph, pointing to the forest behind us.

"Let's go home, Mom," I said.

Gloria said to me, "You did well. You are very strong and very brave."

"Nice going, kid," said Ralph. "You've got great things ahead."

"You mean it isn't over?" I said.

Gloria and Ralph laughed.

"This part is over," said Gloria.

I grabbed my mom's hand and headed into the trees.

"Our living room is here somewhere," I said.

"Lizzie," my mom said, "have you completely lost it?"

We went around a trunk and pushed aside some branches and spilled out into our living room. We were home. I was so relieved. My dad and Booger were standing in front of the couch.

I went over and hugged my dad. Then get this, I hugged Booger.

I screamed at my dad. "Aren't you going to ask us where we've been?"

My dad looked at both Booger and my mom.

"Is this a joke, Liz?"

"Are you insane?" I said. "We've just been through the Christmas tree. I had to go save Mother from this horrible thing, and it almost got me, too."

"She's sick, Dad," said Booger.

"When did you do this?" asked my dad. "You've been standing right here for quite a while."

"You were asleep," I said.

"Okay," said my dad, raising his eyebrows like I was nuts.

"Everybody stop for a minute," said my mom, "I'm trying to remember something, and it's slipping away."

"You were in this horrible dark thing," I said, "remember?"

She gave me a total blank look.

"This is terrific," I said. "I have the weirdest and scariest thing happen to me in my whole life and no one remembers it or believes me."

My dad said, "We'll talk about it later, Liz. Right now, we have to remember to be on time for your mother's famous pageant."

"What day is it?" I asked.

"Christmas Eve, dumbhead," said Booger.

"I lost a day," I said. "This doesn't make sense."

"Hurry, you guys," said my mom. "Get dressed. We can't be late."

"We're always late," said my dad.

My mom gave him a dirty look.

I was the last one dressed, of course, and the last one out the door. I stopped to look at the Christmas tree. It really was a beautiful tree.

There was the Ralph ornament, dancing his legs off. Right above him was our beautiful Christmas angel.

I said, "It's Gloria! The angel looks like Gloria."

My dad yelled, "Come on, Lizzie. We're late."

"I'm coming," I yelled.

I heard something rustling behind me. I whipped around, half afraid of what I'd see.

It was Ralph and with him was Gloria.

"Merry Christmas," said Ralph.

"Merry Christmas," said Gloria.

"Merry Christmas," I said.